Shakespeare Tales

Romeo & Juliet

First published 2016 by

Bloomsbury Education, an imprint of Bloomsbury Publishing Plc
50 Bedford Square, London, WC1B 3DP

www.bloomsbury.com

Bloomsbury is a registered trademark of Bloomsbury Publishing Plc
Text copyright © Terry Deary 2016
Illustrations © Tambe 2016

A CIP catalogue for this book is available from the British Library

ISBN: 978-1-4729-1786-7 (paperback)

Printed and Bound by CPI Group (UK) Ltd, Croydon CR0 4YY

1 3 5 7 9 10 8 6 4 2

TERRY DEARY

Shakespeare Tales

Romeo & Juliet

Illustrated by
Tambe

BLOOMSBURY EDUCATION
AN IMPRINT OF BLOOMSBURY
LONDON OXFORD NEW YORK NEW DELHI SYDNEY

Contents

Curtain up
Swords and sweat

The actor's tale

The streets of London were so hot they steamed. The smell choked you. Men and women in masks tried to sweep away the filth but it was a hopeless job. They may as well have tried to stop the tide on the Thames from rising.

And in the foul and baking air some people dripped with the sweating sickness. They stumbled and fell in the streets or lurched home to die. No one wanted to touch the fallen victims. Not even the doctors wanted to go near.

The passers-by hurried on and left the dying to the men with carts who came to pick them up. We all wondered who would be next.

Crowds headed for the theatres to watch the plays of young men like Master Shakespeare. For two hours they could watch actors pretend to die. For two hours they could forget about the hot horrors of the streets and alleys.

They could watch plays like Master Shakespeare's 'Romeo and Juliet'. For a penny they could stand and watch the theatre's thrills. Actors died on stage then jumped to their feet, smiling. It was all pretend. I know because I was one of those actors.

I peeked through the curtain and watched the first scene on the streets of Verona...

Young men entered with swords and clubs and daggers drawn. They swirled and twirled round one another like dancers: darting, shouting and snarling as the swords swished.

Some wore cloaks of blue, each marked with a silver letter 'C'. Their enemies wore cloaks of red with an 'M' in gold.

A small man with a beard and a cloak of blue was beaten and bruised. His dagger clattered on the wooden boards, leaving him with no weapon. He cried and moaned and made off with an enemy boot on his behind to help him on his way.

That left the blues one fighter short. So two reds turned on a fat and panting blue who beat them off till sweat ran down his face. A red-cloaked man, with hair as black as any bat, jumped forward and thrust a rusting sword towards the fat man's giant neck. The big man cursed and clutched the wound. He took his hand away all red and sticky wet.

He swayed, he stumbled, then he tumbled forward like a falling tree headed straight towards me. In the shadows I grasped his arm and guided him towards a stool. He grinned. He chuckled. 'Was I good?' he asked.

'You fought like a gallant knight, Master Richard,' I smiled and, with a damp cloth, wiped the red paint off his hand and neck. Then I pulled his cloak and jacket off. His sweat smelled sharp as vinegar.

I dipped my fingers in a pot of

white-lead paint and rubbed it into his cheeks till he was ghastly white. I wiped red powder on his cheeks to make them bright and then I put a horse-hair wig on top of his bald head. I helped him step into a large brown dress with a white apron, then I tied it at the back.

'How do I look?' he asked.

'You look just like a children's nurse,' I said.

He nodded hard. 'That's good. Now fetch me some ale. I'm parched and I'll

not be on that stage again for another quarter hour.'

I had the ale ready. Master Richard always asked for pots of ale when he'd been fighting. He sat down on the stool and watched the battle on stage come to an end.

I'd been an actor since the age of nine, two years before. I'd seen a hundred fights on stage and not grown tired of watching them. I couldn't see them all, though. Between my acting parts I had to help with costumes, wigs and setting up the stage. The five boy-actors in the company had to play the women's parts – women weren't allowed on stage in those far off times when Master Shakespeare was alive.

Now I had my first big chance – the role of Juliet in the play by Master

Shakespeare, 'Romeo and Juliet'. I had a leading part, yet still I had to fetch the ale for giant Richard.

I didn't mind. It stopped me fretting with a fluttering heart as I waited for my turn on stage. Would I forget my lines or step upon my fine blue dress and trip and fall clean off the stage? Or lean too far and topple down as I stood on the balcony? Or lose my long, fair wig or – worst of all – begin to giggle when I lay inside my tomb pretending to be dead?

For I was Romeo's Juliet and every day I would have to die – on some days I would die twice.

I turned to watch the action on the stage.

Act 1

Mother and marriage
The play

The town of Verona in Italy

Prince Escalus, the ruler of Verona, arrives. His guards step in between the fighting men. The Prince, red-faced with rage, cries that he will stop the fighting families battling on the streets.

If they are Capulets (the ones in blue) or Montagues (in red), the next men fighting in the street will face the executioner's axe.

The sulking men do not dare grumble.

They slouch away like dogs with tails between their legs. And in walks Romeo, on his way to meet his mother, Lady Montague. He's sad because he loves fair Rosaline. The problem is that Romeo's a Montague and Rosaline's a Capulet. The Capulets will kill him if he tries to marry Rosaline.

(The ladies in the crowd who watched the play all sighed. The actor, Tom, who played the young man Romeo, was handsome. The women swooned and sobbed real tears when he died on stage each day – and, just like me, on some days he died twice.)

Elsewhere, Count Paris calls on Juliet's father, old Capulet, to ask for Juliet's hand in marriage.

'She's just fourteen,' old Capulet sighs. 'Let's wait for two more years.'

'Younger girls than that get married,' Paris argues.

'Then ask her,' Capulet decides. 'If she says yes then I'll agree. Tonight we have a feast. You'll see her there.'

When Romeo hears about the feast – in the house of his deadly enemies – he tells his friends he has to go. At great events like this they all wear masks so no one will know they're Montagues. They should be safe. And there he'll get to meet the lovely Rosaline. It's danger, maybe even death, but Romeo will be there.

The actor's story

The crowd who watched the play all gasped. Some women cried out, 'Don't go Romeo.' They trembled. But I was trembling too. I knew that when he left the stage I had to enter for the first time. I set my wig straight and took a deep breath. Master Richard bustled past me. He would play my nurse. He called me on. I blinked a little in the mid-day sun and saw five hundred pairs of eyes all watching me. 'How now? Who calls?' I said and so my scene began.

The play

Lady Capulet is fretting. 'Tell me, Juliet,' her mother says. 'What do you think of getting married?'

'I haven't thought about it,' Juliet replies.

'Then think about it now,' her mother goes on. 'Count Paris wants to marry you. He'll be there at our feast tonight. See if you like his looks. And don't forget,' she adds, 'He's very rich.'

The actor's story

I hurried off the stage to change into a rich, pale blue dress that sparkled with glass beads like diamonds. Behind the curtains the musicians waited silently with their fiddles and flutes, oboes, drums and lutes. The curtains opened and they began to play. Every actor and stage-hand, dressed in gaudy doublets or dresses, swirled and pranced and leapt and danced as if that little stage was the greatest ballroom in Verona.

The audience clapped and yelled. I grabbed my mask and ran back the stage and swung around on George's arm – the actor playing my father, Capulet. The only still figure in the crowd was Tom, our Romeo, who held a flaming torch and watched, enchanted, as he saw me dancing there. The music ended with a crash. The

actors and the audience cheered, then
settled down to see what happened next.

The play

Romeo sees Juliet and asks a servant who the lovely girl is; all thoughts of Rosaline are suddenly gone from his head. But someone else is listening. The vicious young Capulet from the street fight – the one with bat-black hairt – has heard poor Romeo speak. This is Juliet's cousin, the wild and fierce Tybalt. He reaches for his knife. 'A Montague,' he cries to old Capulet. 'Our enemy. That villain, Romeo.'

'Leave him be,' the old man says. 'He's doing no harm. Say nothing.'

'I'll make him pay,' young Tybalt hisses.

'Not in my house,' Capulet says and Tybalt stalks away to plot revenge.

Romeo puts down his torch and joins the dance. He takes the hand of Juliet and begs a kiss.

Nurse bustles in and says that Juliet's mother want to see her. 'Who's her mother?' Romeo asks.

'Why, Madam Capulet,' the nurse replies.

And Romeo feels pure misery. 'She is a Capulet? I love the daughter of my enemy?' he moans as his friends take him from the feast.

When Juliet returns she asks her nurse, 'Who was that young man?'

Nurse replies, 'His name is Romeo, and a Montague. The only son of your great enemy.'

And Juliet feels the same despair as Romeo.

The actor's story

I left the stage and squeezed tears from my eyes. I heard the watching crowd sigh, all together, like one person.

I pushed through the actors who were struggling to change out of their feast costumes and dress for their next scene. I pulled the glittering dress over my head and handed it to the costume man. I was wearing a nightdress underneath, ready for the next scene. I walked up the candle-lit stairs at the back of the stage and stood on the balcony, behind the curtain, and waited to enter. I stepped out into the sunshine and acted a scene that was supposed to be in moonlight...

Act 2

Monk and meddle
The play

Romeo climbs the orchard walls and creeps into the Capulets' garden. He stands there hidden, hoping to catch a glimpse of Juliet. She steps out onto her balcony and sighs like a summer breeze. 'Oh, Romeo. Why are you called Romeo? A Montague. It's just your name that is my enemy.'

If Romeo's caught inside the garden then the Capulets will kill him. Yet when he hears her speak he moves out of the shadows, saying, 'For you, my love, I'll change my name.'

'If you are honest – and wish to marry me – then send a message in the morning. Tell me where and when we'll marry and I'll come to you,' the girl says.

The young man makes a promise that he'll send a message with her nurse at nine tomorrow morning. Nurse starts calling Juliet and the lovers have to part. They say a long goodbye and Romeo hurries off to see a priest.

He knows a monk called Friar Lawrence and will try to persuade the friar to marry

them in secret. 'My heart is set on the daughter of rich Capulet. We hope that you can marry us today.'

The monk is shocked – he tells the young man that he hardly knows the girl. But Romeo does not give up. At last, Friar Lawrence says he'll marry them. The fighting families will have to make their peace if Romeo weds a Capulet. All Verona will be glad to see the hatred and bloodshed end.

But nothing ever goes to plan. That black-haired Tybalt's in a rage. He wants revenge on Romeo for daring to come to last night's feast. And Tybalt is a killer with a heart of ice.

Romeo meets Juliet's nurse and says he'll marry Juliet that very afternoon. Nurse goes off to give the girl the happy news. Juliet is to go Friar Lawrence's cell to be married to Romeo.

The actor's story

I loved that scene. Mr Shakespeare wrote it so well. The nurse arrived home. As Juliet, I asked her if she had a message from Romeo and she teased. She found a dozen things to say before she told me, at last, what I wanted to know. That Romeo was waiting for me.

The watching crowds knew what the message was. They loved to watch me rage and stamp my feet in tiny tantrum. They laughed to see me cry. So much laughter. So many tears would come soon after. That laughter was a flash of sun before the storm.

That day when I played Juliet the sun was hot. The theatre was a great circle of wood that held the sweating air like a copper pan holds water. The watching crowd supped ale to cool themselves, ladies in the in the shaded box seats flapped their fans like moth-wings, and everyone waited for the first of many deaths on stage.

The heat was perfect for this play. The wild young Montagues and Capulets were wandering the streets, restless in the heat of the fierce Verona sun, their linen shirts itching and making hot tempers boil over. I watched as enemies edged towards that final fight...

Fight and flight
The play

So Romeo and Juliet marry in secret. But sadly, the story doesn't end there.

Juliet's black-haired cousin roams the streets to seek out Romeo. To fight. To kill the Montague who dared to feast last night at Juliet's house. It is a crime and Romeo must pay.

But it is Romeo's cousin, Mercutio, who meets the raging Tybalt first. Swords flash

and ring as Tybalt and Mercutio clash. Blue cloak and red are thrown back as rivals fly at one another.

Poor Romeo is horrified. Mercutio is his cousin, but Tybalt is his cousin now too, by his marriage to Juliet. He tries to step between the two and that is when the cruel calamity strikes.

Tybalt thrusts his sword under Romeo's arm and stabs Mercutio in the chest. Romeo's bleeding cousin falls onto the dusty street to die. 'Why did you step in?' Mercutio sighs. 'You killed me, Romeo,' he moans and lies back lifeless.

Romeo draws his sword and flies at Tybalt in a fury, killing Juliet's cousin in revenge. The Montague men drag him

from the street. The Prince has warned that fighters will be executed. Romeo must leave Verona now and not waste one second.

When Juliet hears the news of Romeo's fight and flight she thinks her life is ended. Her nurse promises Juliet that she'll make plans for Romeo to come that night for one last visit. 'He is hid at Lawrence's cell,' she tells the weeping Juliet.

'Take this ring to show I care and send him here to say goodbye,' says Juliet

So Romeo gets to meet his Juliet and hopes that one day he might be forgiven. Perhaps he can come back and they can live together. But for now he has to ride to some other city – any city but Verona.

They say goodbye but live in hope. They do not know that Juliet's father has his own plan. Old Capulet has never seen his daughter so upset – he thinks she's torn apart by Tybalt's death. He doesn't know it's Romeo she's crying for.

His plan to make her happy is quite simple. He tells Count Paris that Juliet will marry him in two days' time. When her mother brings the news, young Juliet refuses. Her father is so angry he says he'll throw her from his house.

'Hang thee, you young baggage,' he bawls. **'I tell thee what: get thee to church on Thursday, marry Paris, or never look me in the face again.'** When Juliet tries to argue he shouts,

'Speak not. Reply not. Do not answer me.' He strides out of her room and leaves her shaking in the arms of old Nurse.

'I'll go and see old Friar Lawrence,' Juliet tells her nurse. 'I'm sure he'll find some way to help me and my Romeo. If he can't help, I'll kill myself'

The actor's story

The shouting of the actor was an act. I knew that James, who played the part of Juliet's father, was quite a gentle man. Yet when he shouted spittle flew out from his mouth and sprayed my face. I really felt afraid.

We left the stage and I felt weary to my bones. We had a short break while the people in the theatre bought more drink and nuts and babbled to each other about the news. Word spread. The plague was back in London.

Victims swelled and burned with fever, then they died in days.

A ragged man in the audience coughed. The people near him moved away and someone muttered 'plague'. They pushed the man towards the door and out into the sun-baked street. The play went on, the

way plays do, and soon the crowd forgot
about the coughing man...

Act 4

Poison and plague
The play

When Juliet arrives to meet with Friar Lawrence she finds Count Paris there. He's making plans to have the Friar bless their marriage.

At last Count Paris leaves and promises he'll see Juliet in two days' time when they are wed. Juliet groans, **'O, shut the door! Then weep with me. I am past hope, past cure, past help.'**

She says she'd rather die than marry that young lord. And that gives Friar Lawrence an idea. **'I do spy a kind of hope,'** he says. 'It will be dangerous,' he warns.

'I'll do anything you say, rather than marry Paris,' Juliet cries.

The Friar nods and reaches for a dark green glass bottle from a shelf. 'Go home. Be merry. Say that you agree to marry – tell them you are happy. Go to bed then drink this liquid. You will seem to die. Your pulse will stop. The roses in your lips and cheeks shall fade. You will go stiff and cold.'

'But I'll not die?' the trembling girl breathes and clutches at the bottle.

'The wedding will be stopped. They'll take you to the Capulet family tomb and leave you there. In two days you will wake again. Romeo will let you out and take you off to some safe town.'

'I'll fall asleep and wake inside a tomb?' she whispers.

'Romeo will be there, never fear,' the Friar says.

'Don't mention fear,' fair Juliet laughs. 'Love will give me strength, and strength will help me do this.'

'I'll write a letter now to Romeo and send a friar with it. I'll tell him all about our plot,' says Friar Lawrence.

'Goodbye, dear Friar,' Juliet sighs and goes off, fearless, to her death bed.

The actor's story

After that I had a short scene with my father, old Capulet. He is so happy at Juliet's plan to marry Paris that he says she and Paris will marry tomorrow morning. I changed into Juliet's night clothes that would also be her burial clothes. Richard helped me smear white chalk on my face until I looked as pale as death and then I stepped back on the stage. In the warm afternoon sun I had to act as cold as any grave.

The play

Juliet tells her nurse and mother, **'Leave me to myself tonight.'** And, when they're gone, she takes the dark green bottle from under her pillow.

Now the moment's come to take the drug, her mind is filled with fears. 'What if the Friar gave me poison that will kill me? What if I wake before Romeo comes and I find myself alone in that dark tomb? The reeking flesh of long-dead Capulets will smother me. What if I wake alone, lying next to cousin Tybalt's corpse, and see

his ghost and die of terror in that tomb?'
She shudders, tears the stopper from the
bottle and swallows down the drug saying,
'Romeo, I drink to you.'

The actor's story

The back of the stage was like a small house – the 'tiring house' we called it. My bed was set in a small opening in the wall. I drank from the empty bottle and closed my eyes. I heard the watchers gasp as I fell back onto the bed and lay there, still as some Egyptian mummy.

Of course the play went on, and I could not stand up and walk away. So the curtains closed and hid me.

The play

On the morning of the wedding day the nurse arrives to wake the sleeping Juliet. She finds her still and cold. Her wedding party becomes her funeral party.

Friar Lawrence sees her safe inside her tomb and sends a message off to Romeo. The plot is working. What can go wrong?

Act 5

Tomb and tragedy
The play

Romeo frets and waits for news. But the letter from Friar Lawrence doesn't reach him – the letter telling him that Juliet's just sleeping. Instead a servant from Verona arrives and tells Romeo the news that everyone believes – that Juliet is dead and in the Capulet tomb.

Now Romeo feels his life is over. He decides he'll go home and enter Juliet's tomb. There he'll take his own life and he'll be at rest with her. **'My Juliet, I will lie with thee tonight,'** he promises and hurries to Verona.

Friar Lawrence makes his way to the tomb to open it. **'In just three hours fair Juliet will awake,'** he says. He will get there too late.

Count Paris comes to lay his flowers on Juliet's grave. But Romeo arrives and steps towards the tomb. Paris draws his sword and cries, 'Young Montague you're banished. You must die.'

'I must indeed, now go away and let me die with Juliet.'

The young men fight and Romeo stabs the Count. As he lies dying Paris says, **'Oh, I am dying. If you're merciful, open up the tomb. Let me lay with Juliet.'**

And Romeo promises he will.

The actor's story

Tom, the actor playing Romeo, pulled the curtains on the tiring house. I was lying on the bench and trying not to breathe. More white chalk had been powdered on my face — it drifted in my nose and made me want to sneeze.

The audience was silent now as Romeo dragged Paris to lie beside me — the girl he thought was dead. One sneeze from me the whole play would be ruined. And still it tickled. I don't know how I held my breath so long.

The play

Romeo pulls a bottle from his pouch – a deadly poison that will snuff his life like a candle in hard rain. 'The drugs are quick,' he says and then falls dead.

Moments later Juliet wakes to discover the terror of the tomb with two fresh bodies lying there – poor Paris and her husband, Romeo.

She finds the poison bottle but it's empty. **'Oh unkind husband. You've left no friendly drop to help me join you.'**

It's then she sees the knife at Romeo's belt. **'O happy dagger, rust here and let**

me die.' She pulls it out and thrusts it into her heart.

The families of the lovers hurry to the scene. Too late, they see what all their hate has done. Old Montague promises to build a golden statue of Juliet, and Capulet promises to build one of Romeo.

The play ends with the Prince's prayer for the lovers:

'For never was a story of more woe,
Than this of Juliet and her Romeo.'

Epilogue

The actor's story

There was a moment's silence. Then the clapping started. The audience began to cheer and the actors all began to smile. So many dead people but it was all a play.

We stepped forward and took our bows in groups of two or three or four. Then, last of all, I rose up from the bench that was my tomb, joined hands with Tom who played Romeo, stepped forward and dropped into a curtsey, as if I were a girl.

The shouts became a roar for me. It made my eyes prick with tears. That glorious

summer day, there on the stage, the rich and poor all cheering for me. It faded as a man stepped from the tiring house and strode across the stage.

It was the writer, Master Shakespeare himself. He rested a hand lightly on my shoulder and whispered, 'Marvellous, young Sam. I wrote the words but you made them live.' I thought my heart would burst with pride and leave me as dead as Juliet.

Then the writer stood at the edge of the stage, raised a hand and the crowd grew silent. 'You'll all have heard, the plague has come to London once again.' The audience's happy smiles slipped off their faces. 'The council says plague spreads when crowds come close together. To stop the spread they have ordered all the theatres to close. That was the first show of "Romeo and Juliet". It may be the last for a while.'

The grim and grumbling crowd shuffled out and Master Shakespeare turned to us. 'Thank you all,' he told the actors. 'I will see you here again as soon as the plague is gone. Master Burbage will pay you for today's show.'

'How will we eat when that is gone?' the giant Richard asked – eating was important to him.

Will Shakespeare shrugged. 'You'll have to find another job till the theatre opens again.'

For me that meant back to my father to help him make fine saddles. I dreamed of the days when I'd play Juliet again and stand in the cheers that were warmer than that summer sun.

I never did. That month the sweating sickness took my father. I had to take over his workshop to keep my mother and my little sisters. I never returned to the stage.

Seventy years on – women are allowed to act these days – but I'll never forget my moment in the sun as Juliet with her Romeo.

Did you know?

Everyone's heard of Romeo and Juliet even if they've never heard of Shakespeare. They are Romeo and Juliet.

William Shakespeare wrote plays but he didn't always think of the stories. In 1562 (two years before Shakespeare was born) a poem was written called *The Tragical History of Romeus and Juliet*. The poem was very popular and Shakespeare took the story to make his own Romeo and Juliet.

In the poem, Romeus thinks Juliet is dead so he drinks poison.

So is the poison spread throughout his bones and veins.

Since Shakespeare's play was first performed there have been many other stories of hopeless love between two young people who should be enemies. A 1970s film was made at a time when Russia and America were close to war. A Russian boy and an American girl fell in love. The film was called Romanov and Juliet.

There is also musical about two lovers from rival street gangs in New York; it was a singing and dancing Romeo and Juliet called *West Side Story*.

So there's nothing new about taking the story and presenting it in a different way... as a poem, as a play, as a film, as a musical play.

In the musical the hate is not between two families. It is between two gangs from New York – the Sharks and the Jets. Instead of Romeo and Juliet we have Tony and Maria. In Shakespeare's play Romeo kills Juliet's cousin. In *West Side Story* Tony kills Maria's brother. Of course Maria's friend, Anita says that Maria must forget all about Tony. After all he killed her brother. She should find a boyfriend from their own gang. Maria should stick to her "own kind". Of course Tony IS her kind because he is a human being. Tony (Romeo) is killed.

Maria (Juliet) says BOTH gangs killed him. It was their hate that led to his death. But in *West Side Story* Maria (Juliet) doesn't die, unlike in Shakespeare's play.

What next?

A story can be told as a tale, as a play, a movie or a poem or in song.

Why not try telling part of the story of Romeo and Juliet as 4 lines of poetry? Or maybe think of a piece of music you know and write Romeo and Juliet words to fit that tune.

1. Madam Capulet, Juliet's mother, tells her daughter how lucky she is to marry Count Paris (Tip: to the tune of 'Twinkle, twinkle little star'. 'What a truly happy day...'

2. Juliet tells her nurse she has fallen in love with a boy she met at the dance. (Tip: to the tune of Old Macdonald. 'I have seen a boy so fine...')

3. Friar Lawrence tells Juliet to take a drug that will make her sleep so deep everyone will think she is dead. (Tip: to the tune of 'All things bright and beautiful'. 'Take this cup and drink it all...'

4. Their families find Romeo and Juliet dead. They know it was the family hatred that killed their boy and girl. (Tip: To the tune of 'Baa, ba, black sheep'. 'See what all that hate has gone and done...'

Take any tune and any part of the story and have fun with it. Write as many lines as you want. The Tragical History of Romeus and Juliet has over 3000 lines... but there's no need to go that far.

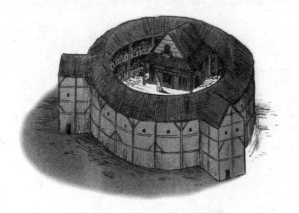

Terry Deary's Shakespeare Tales

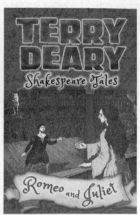

If you liked this book
why not look out for the rest of
Terry Deary's Shakespeare Tales?
Meet Shakespeare and his
theatre company!

World War I Tales

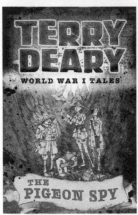

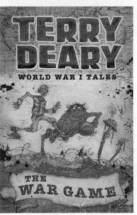

Exciting, funny stories based on real events . . . welcome to World War I!

World War II Tales

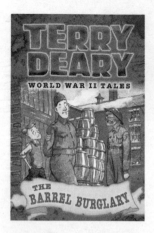

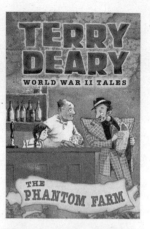

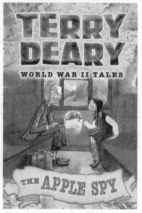

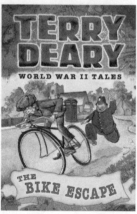

Exciting, funny stories based on real events...
welcome to World War II!